THE CRYSTAL BOWL

THE CRYSTAL BOWL

Australian Nature Stories

J. J. Hall

Illustrated by Dorothy Wall

Angus & Robertson Publishers

JF

This book is dedicated to Eleanor whose appreciation
and encouragement have enriched its contents

ANGUS & ROBERTSON PUBLISHERS
London • Sydney • Melbourne • Singapore • Manila

First published by Whitcombe & Tombs Ltd 1921
This edition by Angus & Robertson Publishers 1981

National Library of Australia
Cataloguing-in-publication data.

Hall, J. J. (James John)
The crystal bowl.

First published: Melbourne: Whitcombe & Tombs, 1921.
For children.
ISBN 0 207 14295 5.

I. Title.

A823'.2

Printed in Hong Kong

CONTENTS

A LARGE CRYSTAL BOWL STOOD IN THE CENTRE OF THE CAVE.

The Crystal Bowl

DEAR, dear me—you never heard such a noise in all your life! The brownies and pixies were calling their little ones from every bush and every tree. The birds had flown down to the pools to wash their faces. The insects were putting on their best frocks. The spiders were brushing the dust from their long legs, and the little native-bears and possums were turning head over heels with joy. You never saw such a fuss! The baby-brownies wore their best bibs, and their mothers and fathers had brushed their hair so well, that they looked quite nice. The tiny pixies tied green ribbons round their new collars and put on their best shoes. You would have thought that all the world was going to a party.

You see, it was this way. The Little Grey Men had found a new light. It was the most wonderful light in the world. They had worked at it for so many years, that you would use up all your tables if you tried to guess how many. How proud they were, to be sure. They had asked all the fairies, the king of the birds, the king of the insects, the king of the animals, and the brownies and pixies to see the new wonder.

Of course, everybody could not get inside the cave where they had made the light. But everybody knew all about it, and, as the Queen of all the Fairies drove to the cave in her beautiful rainbow car, she passed between rows of the little folk who live in the under-world. How they cheered as she passed! Caps flew into the air, and the beetles stood on their heads, and kicked their heels in the air with delight.

Now, a large crystal bowl stood in the centre of the cave. It was filled with something that looked like water, which bubbled, and bubbled, and bubbled, until it seemed that it must boil over. One of the little men took a small box out of one of his large

THE BIRDS HAD FLOWN DOWN TO THE POOLS TO WASH THEIR FACES.

pockets, and emptied the contents into the bowl. The same moment, the cave was filled with a light so bright, that all the guests had to put their hands over their eyes. Some of the baby-brownies cried with fright.

When their eyes became used to the light, they saw ever so many small colored bowls hanging on the walls of the cave. The little men now filled them with fluid taken from the large crystal bowl, and in a little while the cave was like a scene from Fairyland. It was so beautiful that they all clapped their hands.

The Fairy Queen now stood up, and there was instant silence. She praised the little men so much that they looked quite shy. "How did you find such a beautiful light, little men?" she asked. "Oh, it was through Flora," they answered. "Who is Flora?" cried the baby-pixies. "Flora! well—she is Flora!" was the funny answer. The Fairy Queen, however, told the curious little folk that Flora was love—a love that brought light into all hearts. But this love held other things besides joy. Pain was in this love, for unless there is pain, there is no real joy. Hearts must sometimes break to find out what life really means. Eyes must sometimes weep to see clearly the most beautiful pictures, and lips must grow white with suffering before they can speak the words that the world desires so much to hear. But now I am sure all the little ones would like some fun before they go back to their beds. Speak little folk, and tell the little men what you would like best. "A story!" was the reply. The Fairy Queen smiled. She knew well that little people dearly love a story. "Very well," she said. "Each little man will tell you a story, but it must be short, for it will soon be time for all tiny folk to journey to the land of dreams. Now, be very quiet, while the first little man tells you his story."

The Little Grey Man gathered all the baby-brownies and pixies around him, and said: "Have you ever seen 'The Native Fuchsia'?" "Yes—yes!" they replied. "Well, I shall tell you why 'The Native Fuchsia' bends its graceful head."

The Native Fuchsia

THERE was once a pixie who had a very sweet voice. He sang so well that even the birds stopped to listen to his song. Indeed, when he sang all nature seemed to say "Hush!" The leaves kept so still, and the crickets so quiet, that you could almost hear the silence. Now this tiny pixie was very fond of the Native Fuchsia. He would often sit at the foot of a bush, and trill—and trill—and trill, until the flowers bent their heads, and pressed their lips on his hair, to show how much they loved his sweet music. He would then lift up his wee, wee face to the flowers and whisper all kinds of dear things in their soft ears. How they loved to listen to him! They would not miss one note of his voice for all the world! Down, down, their heads would droop to catch even his gentlest murmur. Now you know why the Native Fuchsia bends her graceful head.

"This little pixie was, one day, singing a fuchsia to sleep. Flora, who was passing, heard his sweet music, and walked on tip-toes to the bush to listen. She had brought with her a jackass, who, I am sorry to say, looked very sulky. You see, it was this way. Flora had found the jackass seated on a limb of a fallen tree. His head was right down between his shoulders, and his tail was almost between his legs. Indeed he looked the picture of misery. It seemed that his mate had left him, and flown into the bush. He had had a tiff with her over a worm. She said she had seen it first. He, however, was greedy, and tried to take it from her. His mate gave him such a peck on the head that he grew quite angry and used wicked words. Of course, the worm did not wait. The end of it was that they both lost a meal. and she said she would have no more to do with him. It was, indeed, very sad.

"At first he would not speak to Flora. But Flora was never cross—not even with a grumpy jackass. She sat down beside him, and began to coax, and coax, and coax him, until he sat up and gave her a smile. Then Flora told him to come and see her 'babies.' He opened his eyes, and looked quite surprised, for he did not quite know what she meant. However, he came along, and thus it was that they heard the pixie. The wee chap took hold of Flora's hand, and they walked through the bush until they came to an open space where a lot of small brownies were waiting for her. How they crowded around her, and clung to her skirts. You never heard such a noise in all your days. By and bye, she told them to be quiet, and sat down on some dry fern the brownies had gathered for her.

"The little folk now sat at her feet in a half-circle, and watched her in silence—but with wide-open eyes. Then she called the tiny pixie to her side, and, lifting him on to her lap, told him to sing. The funny, wee mite cuddled close to her warm neck and buried his small face right under her chin. It was a habit he had—and a very dear one. He lay there for a few minutes, and then began to sing.

"Oh, it was so sweet! As he sang the half-circle lost its shape, and the tiny forms stretched themselves on the ground, and closed their round eyes. But their ears were wide open! They saw rows upon rows of lovely trees. Through the leaves of these trees the sun shone. Its beams made the grass beneath to look like a magical carpet of light and shade. Large butterflies with wings of many beautiful colors flitted hither and thither. Birds, dressed in gay feathers, darted here and there. Bush-flowers sprang up everywhere, and gave forth such a sweet scent, that the whole forest seemed filled with perfume. Insects, with garments of all hues, ran in and out of the blades of green grass. The trees swayed ever so gently in the soft summer wind.

"Then the rows of trees changed. The leaves took on tints of red, and yellow, and brown. The shadows grew deeper. The butterflies flew away. The insects lay beneath the blades of grass, or crept quietly into their holes in the earth. The flowers put on heavier clothes, and the wind lost its nice warm feeling. The leaves began to fall—ever so gently, with a music almost as sweet as the song of the pixie. The brownies sat up, and came closer together. Now and then they shivered.

"And now there were no leaves. The light passed away, and only the shadows were left. The birds had flown away. The flowers had tucked themselves away in warm, green overcoats. How cold the wind was! How it whistled through the bare branches. There was now no half-circle. The little folk cuddled closer and closer for warmth. But still the pixie sang on.

"Suddenly the wind changed. It had a feeling of warmth. The trees broke out into masses of blossoms. The flowers threw off their green overcoats and put their beautiful petals in proper order. The birds came back—as if by magic. They joined in the song of the little pixie. Indeed, it was hard, at times, to tell who sang the loudest and sweetest. The lights shone once more, and seemed clearer. Even the butterflies were more beautiful. The wind was as happy as could be, and the whole bush seemed alive with life and joy. Then the pixie stopped! It was all so wonderful that one hardly dared to breathe.

"Then Flora laughed. All at once the bush rang with the glad cries of the little folk, who climbed all over Flora until you could hardly see her. Even the jackass chuckled and chuckled. He sounded so funny, that the pixies rolled over and over in their mirth.

" 'Now,' said Flora to the jackass, 'you are not grumpy. surely?' 'Oh, no!' he replied. 'Come on, little folk,' he said, 'and I shall take you, one by one, up into the big gumtree, and

THE SULKY JACKASS WAS SEATED ON THE LIMB OF A FALLEN TREE.

show you where the honey-pots are!' Flora told him he must be very careful, so he lifted the wee mites up into the branches,

THE JACKASS THOUGHT THAT HE HAD NEVER SEEN ANYTHING SO FUNNY.

and told them to look for the hidden honey. What a good time they had!

"Well," said the Little Grey Man to the brownies and pixies, do you know what the song means?" "Oh, yes!" they replied, "but you have not finished yet!" "Not quite!" said the little man. "I am now going to tell you how the jackass got his laugh. You see, one of the brownies was leaning over the edge of a honey-pot, when one of his mates stole up behind him, and pushed him in. Indeed, he would surely have been drowned, had not the jackass thrust in his long beak and picked him out. The honey fell from him in large drops. Indeed, he was covered from head to foot with the sweet stuff. He tried to walk along the branch, but he stuck at every step. He did look funny! The brownies laughed so much that some of them nearly tumbled off the tree.

"The jackass thought that he had never seen anything so funny. He put back his head, and went into such peals of laughter, that the leaves shook again. His mate, who had returned to see the fun, joined in the mirth, and the whole forest trembled with the most joyous laughter the world has ever heard.

"Now," said the Little Grey Man, "when you hear a jackass laugh, you will know that he is thinking of the little brownie who tumbled head over heels into the honey-pot."

"But what became of Flora?" asked a curious little mite. "Oh, she laughed too! Of course, when the jackass carried the brownie down to her side, she tried to clean him, so that his mother would not be angry with him when he went home. But she had to stop again and again, for she really could not keep back her mirth. It would bubble, and bubble over, just like a kettle of water. Indeed, it was a merry time!

"When you see Flora, just ask her why the jackass laughs so much. She will tell you how funny the little brownie looked, and so bubble over with mirth, that I am sure you will laugh too!"

The Emperor Gum Moth

THE brownies and pixies had just put their legs straight out in front of them so that they might not get cramp. Indeed, with their arms stretched well behind them, they looked quite at their ease. They, however, soon sat up when the next little man came along. With their hands clasped around their knees, they waited to hear his story. At that moment a brownie fell back, and made such a funny noise that the little folk could not make out what was the matter. The little man rushed to the brownie's aid, and caught hold of him by the heels, and stood him on his head. He then thumped the wee fellow's back so hard that the little people thought the brownie's back must break. But a pepper-berry flew out of his mouth, and he was soon quite right. You see, he had brought a branch of the pepper-tree with him into the cave, and was sucking the pretty red berries. One of the berries stuck in his throat, and he might have choked if the little man had not thumped it out. But his eyes were full of tears, and he swallowed and swallowed for a long time before he was quite well.

The little man now held up the branch of the pepper-tree, and asked the brownies and pixies if they could see anything. The little folk looked and looked for a long time. No, they could not see anything except the berries. At last the brownie who had brought in the branch cried out, "There is a caterpillar on one of the twigs. He was asleep when I broke off the branch, and I did not care to wake him."

"Well," said the little man, "one of our number once injured the wing of an Emperor Gum Moth whose wings he was painting.

Of course he was punished for his lack of care. Still, there was the Moth to be considered, and the Queen of all the Fairies desired to comfort the Moth for its injury. She therefore told the Moth that she would grant her what she desired. Now, it was a risky thing, even for the Fairy Queen to do, for we are apt to make an unwise use of our desires. The Emperor Moth, however, showed her wisdom by asking for a very wise favor. She asked the Queen of all the Fairies to destroy the fly that preyed on so many of her kind. This fly was in the habit of piercing the body of the caterpillar of the Emperor Moth, laying an egg in the wound, and so causing a grub to grow. This grub fed on the body of the caterpillar, and, in the end, caused its death.

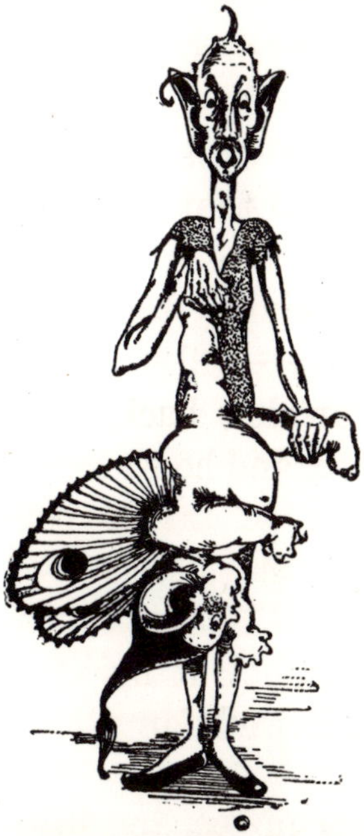

THE LITTLE MAN STOOD THE BROWNIE ON HIS HEAD.

"The Queen of all the Fairies looked rather sad over the request. 'You see,' she said to the Emperor Moth, 'although I should love to do as you desire, there is a greater power than mine. Mother Nature, who rules all things—even fairies—has ordered that the fly should live. But I shall help you in another way. To your children and your children's children I shall give the pepper-tree. Its lovely leaves will help to protect them from their enemies. There will be less fear for their safety, and such knowledge, I am sure, will surely bring you greater comfort.'

"Well, the Fairy Queen was so delighted with the unselfish desire of the Emperor Gum Moth, that she resolved to reward such wisdom. She therefore led the moth to the fairy treasure-house, and showed her the wonderful Jewels that were stored there. The moth was almost beside herself with delight, for she had never seen such beauty. The Queen of all the Fairies now chose a number of the loveliest jewels, and said: 'Dear Emperor Gum Moth, your caterpillar shall always wear these gems as a token of my good will towards you. However, to make them still more beautiful, you must take them to the Seven Little Grey Men, who will make their beauty live for ever, and adorn you as nothing else in the wide, wide world has even been adorned.'

"The Emperor Moth murmured her thanks for the lovely gift, but the Fairy Queen noticed that the moth's gaze was fixed on four large lustrous jewels that had been put in a place by themselves. The Queen of all the Fairies smiled. She knew how desirable these jewels were. 'Ah!' she said, 'I know what is in your mind, my dear friend, but I may not give you these jewels. They must be won! Some golden deed must be done to win them! However, I shall leave them in the charge of the Seven Little Grey Men for a little while. Should you win them, well—I shall give them to you with the greatest delight!'

"The Emperor Moth carried the jewels to the Little Grey Men, who, with great care, placed them in the wonderful crystal bowl. Then, almost before the moth was aware of the fact, she was ever so gently covered with a cream-colored mantle. When the mantle was removed, lo and behold, in place of the moth appeared a large caterpillar. On the back of the caterpillar was placed a robe of a beautiful pale blue color. You see, the little men had gone out early one clear spring morning, and gathered the tint from the morning air. It had been mixed with crystal dew, and was so clear, that you almost seemed to see right through it. Along the sides of the caterpillar were fastened two narrow yellow bands. The color had been taken from the buttercups in the field, and, of course, rain could never wash it out.

"The jewels were now carefully removed from the bowl. On the shoulders of the caterpillar were fixed several rows of lovely

IN A LITTLE WHILE, THE WHOLE BODY APPEARED, AND THEY THEN SAW A WONDERFUL MOTH.

sapphires. Have you ever watched the sea on a warm day in the Summer? Well, you know how blue it looks. These sapphires were just like the sea. Along the body were placed rows of rubies. You have seen, I am sure, a red glow on the distant ranges at nightfall. It is the after-glow of a bush-fire, and looks so red and bright that you at once think of jewels. Well, these rubies were like so many tiny fires.

THEY GENTLY KNOCKED AT THE DOOR OF THE LITTLE BROWN HOUSE.

"The caterpillar was now put on the branch of a pepper-tree and sent off to sleep. While it slept, the Seven Little Grey Men gathered the deep brown tint from the Autumn leaves, and spun it into threads as fine as silk. With loving care, they wrapped the threads, one by one, around the caterpillar, until he was completely hidden inside a little brown house. When a few days had passed, they gently knocked at the door of the little brown house, and it at once began to tremble. The softest sound in the world was now heard, and by and by the door opened. First of all a brown head was poked outside the door—then a brown leg—and then another. In a little while, the whole body appeared, and the little men then saw a wonderful moth. The wings unfolded bit by bit, until they were outstretched to the warm, dry air. Filled with a delight that no pen can write, the

THE LITTLE GREY MEN PAINTED THE WONDERFUL COLORS ON THE BODY OF THE CATERPILLAR.

moth quivered in the glorious sunshine—and, the next moment, had flown out into the beautiful world. As hour after hour sped, she gloried in the joy of life; but, mixed with her joy, was the ever-present desire for the four wonderful jewels that had still to be won. However, as often happens, our blessings come when we least expect them.

"Now, there was a small boy named Will, who lived on a farm that lay a few miles from the limestone cave. The farm was a small one, and the boy's parents were poor. His father was forced to add to his small income by selling timber on the farm. Will often helped his father in this work, and at times drove a team of four bullocks into the township. He was, of course, a bush-boy, and was able to handle stock. It was therefore no great feat for him to drive a team of bullocks.

"Will had, one afternoon, taken a load of wood to a regular customer, and was returning homeward, when an unusual noise attracted his attention. He soon located the sound, and was surprised to see a large fox entangled amongst the timber that was strewn by the side of the road. The animal had been caught in a trap, but the large iron pin that held the chain had yielded to the frantic struggles of the fox. In its headlong flight, the animal had dragged the trap into the timber. The loose chain and pin had caught in the limb of a fallen tree and held fast.

"The boy could hardly be blamed for allowing his excitement to overcome his caution. His fault really lay in the fact that, in spite of all warnings, he was, at the time, in the cart. Bullocks should always be driven on foot, and Will suffered the penalty that ever attends the lack of care. The team, swerving slightly, pulled the cart over a large stump. Before the boy could stop the animals, the cart was overturned, and the driver thrown out. Will tried to roll clear of the cart, but one of the wheels jolted heavily on to his leg, and pinned it to the ground. He had sufficient presence of mind to stop the bullocks, but all efforts to free himself failed. The animals soon grew restive. Their impatient movements caused the lad such pain that he fainted.

"The Emperor Moth, returning from his long flight, saw the boy lying still and white by the roadside. She rested a while to think what she should do. Her mind was soon made up, and off she flew like a ray of light. On and on, and ever on she flew, until she saw several boys who were coming from school. She flew in front of them, above them, around them, and risked all danger to lure them along the track that led to the injured lad.

"Drawn on, in their attempts to catch the moth who was so daring, the boys at last came upon the overturned cart. With the skill of bush-children, they placed a stout limb of a tree beneath the wheel, and soon freed the sufferer. Help was quickly found, and Will taken back to the township, where the local doctor attended to his injuries. No bones had been broken, but a bolt on the rim of the wheel had bored into the boy's leg, and badly torn the flesh.

"The Emperor Moth now made all haste to the Seven Little Grey Men. She was surprised to see, in the cave, the Queen of all the Fairies. Of course the Fairy Queen knew the golden deed that had been done, and was waiting for the moth to arrive. Everybody in the cave was very happy. Goodness and self-sacrifice always bring their own reward.

"The Queen of all the Fairies ever so gently dipped the four large jewels into the crystal bowl, and when she lifted them out they seemed to be alive. She now, with the greatest care, fixed them in the wings of the moth. Should you desire to see these wonderful gems, you must quietly approach the Emperor Gum Moth, and you will then see them shining on her glorious wings. But do not touch her, for she is very fragile, and you might dim the lustre of her precious and priceless jewels."

The Clematis

THE last echo of delight that followed the story of the Emperor Gum Moth had hardly died away, when a sudden hush fell upon the brownies. Loud and clear rang out the "good-night" call of the birds to the little folk. They could not understand it. The birds had gone to bed hours ago. But in their own way, they were wise little people—and they waited. Again the call rang out, even more clearly and loudly. A pixie—the smallest of the tribe—rose slowly to his feet, and walking towards one of the little men, placed a tiny hand on his sleeve, and gazed into his face. The little man smiled, the Queen of all the Fairies smiled, the brownies and pixies smiled, while the rest of the little folk of the underworld wondered. What did it all mean?

The Little Grey Man, still smiling, sat down amongst the little people, and placing the wee, wee pixie on his knee, said: "Well, little folk, what bird bade you 'Good-night'?" "The Blue-cap!" was the instant response. "Quite right! Now I shall tell you why I gave you the 'Good-night' call of the Blue-cap."

"The little Blue-cap had a friend whom he loved very much. This friend was a boy called Possie. Why he was called Possie I am unable to tell you. Perhaps, in his earlier years—when he could just speak—he had called someone or something by that name, and his parents had given him the title.

"Now, Possie was ten years of age, but he was so big that he might easily have been taken for a lad of fourteen. He could ride any horse, swim with the ease and grace of a platypus, and swing a light axe with astonishing skill. He knew a lot about sheep and cattle, and could mend a wire fence as well as most men. But, sad to say, his mind, as far as lessons were concerned, was a blank.

"Governesses had come and gone like the seasons. After he had pushed a long-suffering lady-help into the bath, it was resolved that he should be placed in the hands of a tutor. School was exciting for the first week. After Possie had received a sound thrashing from his teacher, and had been dropped into a prickly-pear bush for impudence, he became a better and a wiser boy. You see, he was not a bad boy at heart, but he needed a stern hand over him. Indeed, Possie was a strange mixture. A sad story would bring large tears into his beautiful brown eyes, and a caress change him into a delight. At other times, he could be very cruel. His worst cruelty was duck-fishing. He would bait a strong pin with a small piece of meat, and throw the line over the fence near an unfortunate duck. The bait was, of course, swallowed at once, and the bird hauled over the fence.

THE BAIT WAS SWALLOWED AT ONCE AND THE BIRD HAULED OVER THE FENCE.

"This strain of cruelty in Possie's nature gave his parents much anxiety. Cruel boys often become cruel men. However, there was so much good in the boy, that Nature, who is the mother of all good, resolved to save him from turning into an evil man. As you know, pain is often the only way to cure wicked habits.

It hurts—yes, very, very much, at times, but it cleanses the body, and purifies the mind from evil thoughts.

"Possie was sent a sickness that attacked his lungs. For several days he knew nothing. It seemed as if he must die. However, as the days passed, he became slightly better, but it was weeks before he was out of danger. He was then carried out on to the wide verandah that ran round the house, and placed on a couch in the sun. He was too weak to move, and looked so thin and white, that you would never have believed he was once a strong, healthy boy. At this time, the Clematis, which covered the verandah, was putting on its fluffy garments, and the air was so clean and fresh, that Possie's face took on a healthier tinge, and he began to eat with more zest.

"At the same time, each day, a Blue-cap visited him. Perched on the Clematis, the bird would talk to him about its family, the weather, and all sorts of things. Possie became quite fond of him, and, when the bird was late, would fret, and fret, until the Blue-cap appeared. By and bye the Blue-cap was tempted to eat the crumbs that the boy scattered near his couch. As time went on, the little bird often perched on the railing at the foot of the couch. There he would sit and chatter—chatter—chatter, until you would have thought he would surely have talked his head off. His funny tail, standing straight up, helped to give him such a comical look, that Possie often laughed at him. Now laughter is the best medicine in the world, and the boy began to improve quickly. His cheeks became quite healthy-looking, and his hands grew fatter, browner, and stronger.

"Possie's mother was very glad to see that her son enjoyed the company of his tiny bird-friend. She pointed out to the boy that the Blue-cap had given him so much of its company because he had been kind to the bird, and had shown it so much love and attention. And so she taught Possie, through the Blue-cap, that

THE LITTLE MEN CREPT TOWARDS POSSIE'S PILLOW AND STROKED THE BOY'S CLOSED EYELIDS.

cruelty only brings punishment in its train, while kindness and love bring goodness and sympathy.

" 'Mother,' said Possie one day, 'isn't the Clematis beautiful?'

THE BLUE-CAP TOLD THE LITTLE GREY MEN.

'It is,' replied the boy's mother. 'I wonder how it is that it grows so fluffy?' 'Why not ask the Blue-cap?' said his mother; 'I am sure he will tell you.' 'Very well,' laughed the boy, 'I shall do as you wish.'

"Now, although Possie thought, of course, that it was not possible for the bird to tell him about the Clematis, yet the

THE SPIDER WOVE HER FINEST SILKEN THREADS AROUND THE WEE, WEE MITE.

answer came. The Blue-cap told the Little Grey Men, and one warm afternoon one of the little men visited the boy, who was lying on his couch on the verandah. The sun had made him sleepy, for he was still weak. The little man, ever so quietly, crept towards Possie's pillow, and stroked the boy's closed eyelids, until he journeyed away to the Land of Dreams. Then the little man, in the softest of whispers, answered the question the lad had asked the Blue-cap. Now, little folk, listen silently while I tell you what the Little Grey Man whispered.

"A long, long time ago, a tiny baby-brownie was born into the world. He was a dwarf amongst brownies. Indeed, so small was he, that when his mother put him down to rest a big stick had to be stuck in the ground beside him, otherwise he would have been lost for ever. He was the never-ending subject of talk amongst the little folk, whose wide eyes grew wider than ever in their efforts to see him. The fairies were never tired of coming to see him. They held him in their arms so long and so often, that his mother at last became quite jealous of their attentions. The Queen of all the Fairies said she had never seen anyone like him, and was so interested in him that she placed him in the centre of a flower of the Clematis, and told a small spider to look after him.

"As the baby brownie lay in the centre of the star-shaped flower, the spider thought that she had never seen anyone so beautiful. She therefore set to work, and wove her finest silken threads, from petal to petal—layer after layer—until she had woven a wonderful mantle that kept the wee, wee mite carefully protected from harm. You should have seen the wonderful mantle when the morning dew glistened upon it. It was like ever so many diamonds that sparkled in the sunshine. The Fairy Queen was quite delighted. She praised the spider, who blushed and thrilled with pleasure.

"Of course, the time came when the baby-brownie had to be taught how to be useful. But the Fairy Queen did not intend that the beautiful mantle should be wasted. Nothing is ever wasted in Nature. Besides, the flower begged that she should be allowed to keep it in memory of her tiny guest. The Queen of all the Fairies, after a little thought, decided that the request of the flower should be granted. You see, the Clematis had been very kind, and kindness deserves every reward.

"The Queen of the Fairies, with most tender care, untied the delicate threads, and wound them, one by one, around the arms of the Clematis until it looked like a silken star. Then she ever so gently ran her fingers over the silken threads, and they at once burst into thousands of fluffy wisps. These wisps were so like delicate feathers that the little folk, who were eagerly watching the Fairy Queen, cried out, 'Oh, look at the feather-flower!' And that is how the Clematis got its bush-name.

"The spider, however, was grieved that her labor of love should have been so changed. But the Queen of all the Fairies said, 'Do not grieve, dear spider, your mantle shall be called a web.' You shall, for ever and ever, spin this wonderful web, and it shall always be your home. When the whole world gazes upon your beautiful work, it shall marvel at the shape and beauty of the web you have made. Your work shall live for ever and ever, and your effort of love shall be a pattern that shall form the foundation of all harmonious design, strength and loveliness.

"Now you know how the Clematis became so fluffy, and how the spider's web came into the world to delight and amaze mankind.

"Well, little folk, you will be glad to know that Possie still lives amongst all the birds and wild-flowers on his beautiful station. You see, pain always takes something away, but it always leaves something more beautiful in its place. Possie is not cruel now—quite the opposite. He has never forgotten the lesson he learned from the Blue-cap. Again, he never looks at the Clematis without wondering whether the story the little man told him was a dream or otherwise. But we know!"

The Purple Iris

ONCE upon a time—as the story-books say—the Queen of all the Fairies thought she would like to make a new flower. You see, it was like this. News had been brought to her that there had been a very hot summer away in the centre of Australia. The evening sky—to protect herself—had mixed her colors that she might produce a shade that would shield her from the great heat. The shade was a great success—so much so, that all the brownies and pixies and fays were talking about it. Of course, the Fairy Queen said that she would like to have some of it, and sent a pixie to get a little of the color.

Now, the Queen of all the Fairies liked the shade so much that she resolved to make it live for ever. She therefore thought out this plan: One of her guard—a beetle—was sent to the Little Grey Men to see if his armor was strong enough to withstand any attack that might be made upon him. The little men chose their strongest weapon—a ray of violet light—and making the beetle stand in a corner, hurled the ray at him. How he jumped when the ray struck him! The little men now knew that his armor was not as thick and strong as it should be. On taking off his armor, they found that the ray had pierced his suit of mail, and hurt his flesh. It was, I am glad to say, a very slight wound, and they were soon able to heal his injury.

The suit of mail was now dipped in the crystal bowl, and, when it was taken out, was covered with several layers of hard stuff like resin until it was able to withstand the force of the ray.

The armor was then put on the beetle, who returned to his royal mistress.

The Fairy Queen placed the new color near a quiet pool that was hidden amongst the ferns. The beetle was now told to guard it with his life. He was a faithful guard, and kept away all the envious little folk of the underworld, who would certainly have carried off the color had they not been closely watched.

Strange to say, the baby-brownies gave the beetle the greatest trouble. They were too curious for words, and asked all sorts of questions. He had, times without number, to give them gentle nips to keep them at a safe distance from the shade. At last, they tired of their mischief, and asked him to play with them. Of course, he at once said he would do no such thing. Besides, it was hardly the proper thing for a guard of the Queen of all the Fairies to play with baby-brownies.

How they begged—and begged—and begged! In the end, they promised as sure as death that, if he would only play with them for a little while, they would never again go near his precious color. Well, the beetle thought for fully five minutes. He knew that the little folk would keep their promise, so he at last said he would play with them—but not for long.

Quicker than you could ever think, they fell upon the beetle, and dragged him on to a carpet of moss that was spread near by. Forcing him on his back, they seized his legs, and dragged him round and round ever so many times. Two of the brownies, bolder than the rest, sat on his body, and clapped their hands and laughed aloud with joy as they were pulled in a circle around the mossy playground. Faster—and faster—and faster, they rode, until their little heads swam again. Indeed, they became so dizzy, that they tumbled off.

The din brought all their fathers and mothers to the spot. How they laughed, to be sure! Tears ran down their faces, and they held their sides for very mirth. But the beetle enjoyed the

THEY SEIZED HIS LEGS, AND DRAGGED HIM ROUND AND ROUND.

fun ever so much. You see, it was a welcome change to him, and he knew he was doing no harm. The baby-brownies now gathered around him, and asked him to tell them a story. He was, however, quite out of breath, and leaned heavily on his spear that he might recover his wind. One tiny mite, full of mischief, now stole up ever so quietly behind him, and, putting out his foot, kicked away the spear. The beetle, of course, fell to the ground, and struck the earth so heavily that he hurt his nose. The other brownies shrieked with glee. Their mirth made the beetle quite cross, and he walked away in a huff. He had not gone very far, when a cry from the little folk called his attention to a bush that grew near the spot where the hidden pool lay. The beetle told them to keep quite still, and he stole on tiptoes towards the bush. The next moment, a dark body darted away from cover, but the faithful beetle, followed by the brownies, pounced upon it, and pinned it to the ground. They soon saw that it was another beetle that had crept up quietly while the fun was going on. He had dared to steal unawares upon the precious color that he might run away with it. The little folk now tied his legs together, and carried him to a hole in the ground until he should be taken to the Fairy Queen, who would surely punish him for his wicked purpose.

"I never did like that fellow," said the faithful Beetle. "He is the meanest insect I know, but the Queen of all the Fairies will give him what he deserves." "And serve him right, too," said the brownies. "Do you know," the Beetle added, "that he once played me the meanest trick that one beetle can play on another?" "Did he?" replied the little folk. "Yes, indeed!" said the Beetle. "Do tell us all about it!" cried the little folk. "Very well," was the reply, "but you must keep your ears and eyes wide open while I tell you." The brownies promised they would do so.

"You see," said the Beetle, "I had, one day, just finished my dinner, and had rolled up what was left, that I might take it home for tea. Now, my home is on the top of a hill, and I had to roll the ball right up to the top. It was so heavy that, try as I might, I could not get it more than half-way. Indeed, I once slipped, and

THE SUIT OF MAIL WAS DIPPED IN THE CRYSTAL BOWL.

the ball rolled over me. It gave me such a nasty shock, and hurt as well. Just at that moment, this beetle came along, and offered to help me. Of course, I was glad to get his help, and together we rolled the ball of food to the top of the hill. But I was very hot, and was undoing my waistcoat to cool myself, when I noticed the ball move slowly away from me. Would you believe it? but that beetle was trying to roll my ball towards his own home, and right in front of my very eyes."

"How shocking!" said the baby-brownies.

"Yes, indeed!" replied the Beetle; "but I ran after him, and gave him such a push that he rolled to the bottom of the hill. There he lay on his back, with his legs waving in the air. Some ants, who were going home, noticed him, and nipped him so sharply that he turned quickly over and ran away as fast as he could."

At this moment the fathers and mothers of the little folk came along to see why their babies were out so late.

The Beetle said "Good-night" to them, and bade them be good little brownies. He was really sorry when they had gone, but they often came to see him during the days that followed, and brought him all sorts of nice things to eat. Indeed, he grew so fat, that at times, his armor felt quite tight.

Well, the flower, at last, pushed its head above the ground, and grew, and grew, until it became a beautiful purple bloom. The Queen of all the Fairies called it "The Purple Iris," because she thought it looked like a tint she had seen in the rainbow.

Now, before the beetle went away to take up his old duties, he had a long talk with "The Purple Iris." The flower asked him how he had got the wonderful, ever-changing tints in his armor. The beetle was very surprised. You see, he did not know that he gathered the beautiful emerald and golden hues of the moss when the brownies had dragged him around it. The moss had enjoyed the fun, and had spread her hues upon his back because she was pleased with him. She never failed to polish them up as he sped across her magic carpet. Indeed, he shone like the lights you see

I GAVE HIM SUCH A PUSH, THAT HE ROLLED TO THE BOTTOM OF THE HILL.

in the rivers at sunset. Even the Queen of all the Fairies, when she saw his wonderful color, said she must have some of it.

The beetle was now sent to the Little Grey Men, who gathered a lot of the ever-changing hues from his back, and placed them in the crystal bowl. Of course, they did not take the lot, and polished and polished the beetle's back until you could see your face in it.

Now, the Fairy Queen took this ever-changing color from the little men, and spread it over the flower. When she had finished there seemed so many shades of green, and gold, and purple, that you were really at a loss to say what was the right shade. But it was a great success. Now you know how the Iris and the beetle received such wonderful hues.

The next time you see "The Purple Iris," and her friend the beetle, just quietly walk around them, and you will notice that their tints are always changing. Indeed, I am sure that you will never be able to say what the exact color is!

The Spider Orchid

AS another Little Grey Man came into the centre of the cave to tell his story he noticed that one of the tiny folk was still thinking about "The Purple Iris." Perhaps the little mite was wishing that he might see the beetle and ask him for a little of the color that made his back so beautiful. Brownies are very fond of lovely colors, and some of them collect tints from the leaves and flowers. These tints they keep in their tiny rooms, and grow quite angry when anyone tries to take them. Well, the Little Grey Man thought he would play a joke on his small friend. He saw a spider on the end of a thread that hung from the roof of the cave. The little man now broke off the thread, and, walking quietly behind the brownie, made the spider run down the nose of the wee mite. How he jumped, to be sure. He tried to catch hold of it. You should have seen his eyes when the spider at once turned to a flower. Of course, you must know that the little man had this flower hidden in the palm of his hand. But he was so clever, that it really looked as if he had changed the spider into a beautiful bloom. There was a chorus of "Oh!" from every part of the cave, for the flower was the wonderful Spider Orchid. "Do tell us all about it!" cried the tiny folk. The Little Grey Man smiled, and, sitting down on the floor of the cave, began his story.

"The Queen of all the Fairies was once trying a new car that had been made for her in the workshop of the Little Grey Men. It was a wonderful car, and had been woven from threads spun from the rainbow. Your most glorious dream could not imagine the beauty of this lovely car. You never saw such colors. As the car sped along, the moon threw her silver beams upon it and caused it to shine in such a way that all the world thought that there had never before been such a thing of beauty. Hundreds of dainty blue moths pulled the car along. Their wings glistened in the moonlight like pale blue silk when ever so many lights shine upon it. The reins were made of woven moonlight, and, as they trembled in the night air, you could see the beams ripple up and down them like the lights you see on the ocean on a clear night.

"The fairies were quite charmed. They were so happy that they laughed aloud. Indeed, you never heard such delightful laughter—for all the world like the tinkle, tinkle of heath-bells when the evening dew falls upon their petals.

"But, all of a sudden, there was a faint, sad cry. One of the blue moths got her legs caught in the reins, and before she could free them, the reins gave a quick jerk, and down, down, down she fluttered. The Queen of all the Fairies stopped her car, and flew to the aid of the moth. She caught the moth just as the poor little thing was about to strike the earth. With the greatest care, she placed her on a bed of the softest moss, and knocked at the door of a ground-spider who lived near.

"The ground-spider was very sleepy. When he heard the knock at his door, he rubbed his eyes in wonder. You see, it was very late, and, for the life of him, he could not understand what was the matter. However, he got out of bed, and opened his door very, very slowly. He was taking no risks. By-and-bye, he peeped out When he heard the gentle voice of the Queen of all the Fairies, he flung back his door with such a bang, that the baby brownies crept close to their mothers in alarm. The Fairy Queen now told him to spin the finest and softest of threads. When he had finished, the gentle Queen wound it round and round the broken leg of the blue moth until it was firmly held together.

THE QUEEN OF ALL THE FAIRIES STOPPED HER CAR, AND FLEW TO THE AID OF THE MOTH.

"The Queen of all the Fairies thanked the Ground-spider and asked him if there was anything she could do for him. 'Make me beautiful, O, dear Queen, so that all things will not shun me!' he cried. 'Very well,' replied the Queen. She told him to go back to

THE SPIDER AT ONCE TURNED TO A FLOWER.

his little snug house, which was lined with the warmest of silken threads. She then closed the door ever so gently that she might not frighten the little folk.

"Sitting down by the house of the Ground-spider, the Fairy Queen began to sing a most beautiful song. As she sang, all the beetles, all the crickets—indeed, all the life that lives on and under the ground—gathered around her in a circle. The brownies and pixies, far and near, collected in groups, and, as the song

THEY ALL DANCED AROUND THE LOVELY FLOWER, AS IF THEY WOULD NEVER STOP.

rang out, they all swayed from side to side, keeping time with the music, until the whole world seemed to be rocking backwards and forwards. Then the Queen of all the Fairies waved her wand. The door of the Ground-spider now slowly, slowly, slowly opened, and up, and up, and up came a glorious flower that looked for all the world like a wonderful spider. Indeed, it was the Ground-spider who had been changed into a beautiful orchid. All the little folk clapped their hands until the leaves of the trees and bushes trembled with the noise, and the blades of grass tumbled over backwards with very joy. Still singing her song, the Fairy Queen carried the Blue Moth to her home. As she turned around to take a last look at the little folk, she saw the brownies and pixies, the beetles and crickets and spiders, all dancing around the lovely flower, as if they would never stop.

"Of course, the spiders were very proud of their beautiful orchid. They took the greatest care of it. Should you ever be in the fields one fine September evening, just as the sun is going to bed, you will see hundreds and hundreds of dainty blankets that the spiders have thrown over the grass to protect their own flower from harm. But you must be very careful not to destroy these blankets. If you do, the orchid might have a very cold night."

The Lyre Bird

"THIS story is about the King of the Brownies!" said the Little Grey Man. Of course, all the little folk at once turned their heads towards the spot where he sat. He tried to appear as if he did not care whether they looked at him or not. However, I do not think his effort was a great success. You know how shy you feel when everybody looks at you. Your hand fidgets with your collar, and you blush to the roots of your hair, or you catch hold of a corner of your frock, and look at it as if something had happened to it. "Well," said the little man, "there were many brownies who thought that they had equal claims to this high honor. It was therefore decided by the fays that the one who made something really wonderful should be chosen. Of course, the little folk got their brains to work, and busied themselves with making all sorts of things, until some of them became quite cross, and unfit for society. But, you see, it had to be done!

"Now, one brownie wandered off into the thickest part of the bush to think out what he should make. He thought and thought until his head ached. At last, he lay down, and went off to sleep. He was awakened from sleep by a sharp peck on the tip of his nose. To his great surprise, he saw two large dark-brown birds stooping over him. He got such a fright, that he ran off and hid behind a tree. By and bye, he poked his head ever so slowly around the trunk and saw that the birds had hidden behind another tree, and were doing the same thing. It looked so funny that they all laughed. Of course, that put an end to all fear, and they walked towards one another, and began to talk. You see, it was this way! The birds had come to him for help, because their egg had been stolen. They could not find out who had done the wicked deed, but had an idea that a fox who lived in the bush where they had built their nest was the thief.

"The brownie, of course, was very sorry, and, after thinking for a while, said that the nest should be built so high above the ground, that it would be hard for any animal to steal the egg. He was quite willing to show them what they should do, and together they built a mound that was very high indeed. Of course, the birds wished to be quite sure how the mound should be made, and they built a smaller one to help them to remember the brownie's plan. They were so pleased with the result that they danced on top of it until the brownie could not keep his feet still, and you would have laughed at the antics they played.

"The brownie ran about on all fours, and made a noise so like the crack of a whip, that you almost fancied you saw horses. Then he picked up two sticks, and pretended he was sawing wood. It was so like the noise, that the birds said it was wonderful. A sudden bark made the birds run for dear life. But a loud peal of laughter from the brownie chased away their fears. You see, he had barked so well that they thought there was a wild dog about. He then finished up his clever tricks by giving such a wonderful imitation of the calls of the bush, that these calls were answered from all parts of the forest. Indeed, there was such a chorus, that you would have thought that all the birds in the world were talking at the one time.

"The male-bird was so taken by the clever way the brownie mimicked these sounds, that he asked the wee man to teach him. The brownie looked at him for a moment, and said he would do so, if the bird would help him out of a difficulty. He then told the task that had been set by the fairies, and asked the bird's advice.

THE BIRD DANCED ON TOP OF THE MOUND, UNTIL THE BROWNIE COULD NOT KEEP HIS FEET STILL.

The bird looked very serious, but said if the brownie would come the next day, he thought he would have an idea or two for him. The brownie promised he would return, and trotted home.

"The next day, the brownie came back, and waited for his newly-found friend to appear. The time seemed so long, that the little fellow was almost tempted to go home. Of course, the bird was not really more than a minute or two, but, when you are in a great hurry to know anything, waiting is a very hard task. When he appeared, the brownie threw his cap into the air with delight, and barked so like a wild dog, that you could hear all the small bush-animals scampering through the scrub for their very lives.

" 'Well,' said the brownie, 'have you got a plan?' 'Oh, yes!' replied the Bird, 'but you must first of all give me my lesson in mimicry!' 'Very well,' he said, 'come along and I shall teach you all I know!' For a long time, and with great patience for a brownie, the wee man taught his pupil how to imitate all sorts of things. The bird was not exactly a good pupil, but he was very anxious to learn, and, before the lesson was finished, had made very fair progress.

" 'Now,' said the brownie, 'I want to know your plan!' 'First of all,' replied the Bird, 'you must imitate all the calls of the bush!' 'Why?' said the astonished brownie. 'Never mind why!' was the Bird's answer: 'Little brownies should not ask too many questions; besides, it is my plan, and you must do as I say!'

"Of course, the wee man did not care to be treated in such an off-hand way, but he did as he was told. By-and-bye, the trees were alive with all the birds that had answered his calls. 'Now,' said the Bird, 'I want you to ask all the birds for the longest feather they can spare!' 'Why?' again asked the brownie. 'Oh, don't ask me "Why" so many times,' replied the Bird, 'or I shall be cross!' 'Just do as I ask you!' The brownie thought he would like to give his rude friend a piece of his mind. However, he thought better of it, and asked the birds if they would mind giving him one of their longest and finest feathers. They said they did not mind a bit, but they also asked the question 'Why?' The brownie told them to ask his friend, but he was silent on the matter, so they sat round and watched.

"The wee man soon had a number of beautiful feathers, and the ground looked like a most wonderful carpet of lovely colors. The bird now told him to cut the ends of the quills quite close to the feathers. When he had finished the task, he was shown how to pluck off the upper feathers so that the top of the quill should be quite bare. 'Now fit one quill into the other,' said the Bird, 'until all the feathers join.' The brownie did as he was told, and, by and bye, had made one long feather which curved inward at the bottom and outward at the top. 'Very good, indeed,' was the Bird's remark, 'but you must now make another.' The wee man was quite puzzled, but he had not the courage to ask 'Why!' He therefore went on with his task, and, with much care and patience, made another long feather. It was so like the first one, that you really could not tell one from the other.

EACH BIRD GAVE THE BROWNIE A FEATHER.

"But there was no time to sit and admire the work, and the brownie was sent down to the creek that flowed close by to get some pale green reeds. He found a number of very slender reeds

THE WONDERFUL LYRE WAS ADMIRED BY ALL THE BIRDS AND THE LITTLE FOLK.

and brought them to the Bird, along with a handful of wet clay 'Make a cake of clay,' said the Bird, 'and fasten the two long feathers you have made into it, so that the bottom end still has its curve inward, and the top has its curve outward.' The brownie did so. 'Place three reeds in the centre,' was the next order. The wee man, with the greatest care, placed the reeds between the feathers. 'Now,' said the Bird, 'strip the green covers off two of the reeds you have left, and use the white centres to fasten the three reeds together at the top and bottom.' The brownie took the soft white centres of the reeds and bound the whole so neatly and firmly, that, try as he might, the bird could not shake apart any part of it. 'Flatten the clay, so that all you have made will stand up, and cover the clay with the smallest and most beautiful feathers you have left,' directed the Bird. The brownie again did so. 'Walk ten paces away,' was the last order, 'turn quickly, and then tell me what you see!' The wee man stepped out ten paces, and turned like a flash of light. 'Oh!' he cried, 'it's a harp!' Quite right,' said the Bird. 'It is! Oh! isn't it a beauty!' exclaimed the brownie. Indeed, it did look very beautiful. The lovely feathers, fitted so neatly and cleverly, made a wonderful lyre of many delightful colors.

" 'Now,' said the Bird, 'you must not touch it! You must leave the rest to me! Come again to-morrow and you may then take it home with you; but, of course, you must give me another lesson!' 'But why!' said the brownie, with a twinkle in his eye. 'Oh, bother!' was the reply. 'For goodness sake do not ask me that question so often.' The wee man only grinned. 'Wait and see—wait and see!' continued the Bird. The brownie now thanked his friend, and, after a last long look at the lovely harp, ran off home.

"Meanwhile, the Bird visited a family of egrets he knew very well, and got from them a number of their beautiful plumes. With great care, he fastened the graceful plumes to the back of the other feathers, so that they curved outward from either side. Then, by way of a finishing touch, he split an egret feather into two pieces, and placed the halves in the centre so that they curved outward and above the rest. It was, indeed, a wonderful sight, and the Bird felt very pleased with the result. Of course, he could not lift the harp, but he stayed near it all night.

THE BROWNIE WAS SENT DOWN TO THE CREEK TO GET SOME PALE GREEN REEDS.

"When the brownie, the following day, came along to see the bird, he heard a most unusual sound. It was not a song—it was not a bird—it was not even a noise. He stopped and listened. Then he knew. It was really the sound one hears when the stream rushes through the water-reeds and makes them give out their music. But, mingled with the music, was the note the wind utters when the breeze gently sweeps through the leaves—the sound Nature makes when she is happy with her children. Indeed, it was the melody of Nature herself. And where do you think it came from? Why, from the wonderful harp he had made. You see, the wind, blowing ever so gently, was so pleased with the beauty of the lyre, that she gave to the reeds and the lovely feathers the music of the woods, of the trees, of the streams, of the sky itself. No wonder the brownie was charmed!

"At last, the fateful day arrived. The brownies and pixies from far and near gathered together to hear the result. Amidst breathless silence the Queen of all the Fairies arrived. Her fays now brought forward something entirely hidden beneath a beautiful silken cloth, and placed it in the centre of the gazing throng. When the Fairy Queen lifted the shining covering, the little folk saw the lovely harp and burst into loud praise. When the noise had ceased, she told the brownie to come forward, and, touching him with her wand, proclaimed him King of the Brownies. The little folk were now told to keep very, very quiet, and listen. They did so, and heard the wonderful music the wind had given the lyre.

"To the delight of the pixies and the brownies, the Fairy Queen called upon the bird that had thought of the beautiful harp. She praised his skill and wisdom, and said he fully deserved the reward that was now to be given him. He would wear this lyre for ever, so that, when the other birds and the little folk saw it, they would know that the Queen of all the Fairies knew how to reward her subjects.

"The Fairy Queen now told her fays to fix the harp to the body of the bird. When they had done so, she waved her wand over it, and it, at once, became part of the bird's body. But something else happened. The many gay colors of the feathers had gone for ever. In their place was a brown color that was in keeping with the rest of the bird's plumage. You see, the Fairy Queen knew that, although many colors were beautiful in the harp, yet, when the lyre became part of the bird, it would have looked common against the brown feathers of his body. The plumage and lyre were therefore made one color, and a very wise plan it was, to be sure.

" 'Now,' said the Queen of all the Fairies, 'you shall wear the lyre for ever, and shall be known as the "Lyre Bird." The lessons you have learned from the King of the Brownies shall not be lost, for he is now a king. You shall imitate all things, and shall be known and admired as long as the world endures!"

The Wax Flower

THE last of the Little Grey Men now came forward to tell his story. He had hardly begun when a sharp cry of pain from one of the pixies stopped him. The little man looked even more surprised when the pixie tore off his coat, and, putting his hand as far down his back as he could, pulled out a bee. You see, one of the brownies had, earlier in the day, caught one of the busy insects and shut it up in a flower that was just closing its petals for the night. He knew that he had done a mean act, and so had thrust the flower right to the bottom of his largest pocket. But he was a real imp of mischief, and was always getting into trouble.

This little brownie had noticed that the pixie, eager to hear all the little man said, always poked his head forward, and thus left an open space between his neck and his tunic. Full of mischief, the brownie quietly drew the flower from his pocket, and, opening the petal ever so gently, dropped the bee down the pixie's back. The pixie, at once, sat straight up. He, of course, crushed the bee, which badly stung him. Indeed, the pain was so great that he cried out.

The Queen of all the Fairies was not at all pleased. She told the brownie's mother to take him home. It was a pity that he should miss the story, but he should not have been so cruel. There were tears in his eyes as he left the cave, and, you may be sure, he shed more tears when he reached home.

The Little Grey Man felt very sorry for the pixie. Putting his fingers down the tiny fellow's back, he took out the sting. He now placed a cool, green leaf on the sore spot, and, after gently patting the pixie's head, sat down to tell his tale.

"Now, little folk," he began, "it is very strange that there should be a bee in the cave, to-night. My story is about this little insect, who gives us so much sweet honey, and works so hard that we may eat. I shall tell you how the Wax Flower became so beautiful. It was all through the bees.

"Many, many years before you were born, a swarm of bees lived in a hollow-tree that stood in the bush. These bees were very wild. Each bee had, at one time, been driven from home by his fellows, because he was unfit to live with them. One by one, they had become a band that worked great mischief amongst the flowers and blossoms. Even the little folk feared them—as well they might—for these wild bees were very savage. Indeed, they had been known to sting small animals to death.

"The Queen of all the Fairies had grown a beautiful plant. It looked so beautiful that she decided to grow lovely flowers upon it. The fairies were given this task. They had almost finished the blooms, when the swarm of wild-bees made a raid upon them. The fairies, of course, tried to beat them back, but the bees were so savage, that a number of the fays were hurt. When the Fairy Queen heard the sad news, she flew to the hollow tree where the wild-bees lived, and, driving them out of their home, placed them, one by one, in different flowers, and turned them into flying-anthers. Now, I am sure you have seen the slender little stalks in a bloom. On the top of these stalks, you have also noticed a little, yellow shape that looks, for all the world, like a tiny bee. Well, these flying-anthers, as you now know, were once wild and savage bees.

"Of course, the other bees were very, very sorry to hear the terrible disgrace that had been brought upon them. They there-

THE BEES RESTORED THE FLOWERS TO THEIR FORMER BEAUTY.

fore asked the Fairy Queen if she would allow them to restore the flowers to their former beauty. The gracious Queen said that they might do so.

"The bees now set to work to carry out their task. The little, light bees coaxed their flower-friends to give them some of the essence from their petals. This essence they passed from their tiny mouths to the mouths of their elder sisters, who prepared it, and shaped it for use. When it was ready, they stored small pieces of very fine wax beneath their wings, and flew off to the injured blooms. Each bee now put a thin strip of the wax into its mouth. Then, after the wax had been nicely softened, it was gently placed on the petals, the edges joined, and the whole smoothed down, until each petal looked like a beautiful piece of shining wax. The Fairy Queen was very pleased. She even smiled when a bee, losing its hold, slipped down the smooth side of a petal into the bottom of a flower with a thud that shook every bit of its body.

"To show how much she liked the beautiful work of the bees the Queen of all the Fairies ordered all her fays to carry the plants to places where the bright gold was hidden in the earth. She thought it would be a nice idea to show that beauty above the ground should have its equal in beauty below the ground. Now, when you see the Wax Flower in the bush, you will know that something equally precious lies beneath it.

"When the flowers were planted in their new homes, the Fairy Queen took a soft, pink tint from her rainbow-car, and spread it over the Wax Flowers. Then she waved her wand over them, and the lovely color shone out like the beautiful tint on the mountain snow when the sun bathes its face in the early dew of the morning sky."

As the Little Grey Man walked away amidst long and loud cries of delight from the brownies and pixies, the Queen of all the

THE WAX FLOWER WAS CARRIED TO PLACES WHERE THE BRIGHT GOLD WAS HIDDEN IN THE EARTH

Fairies came forward and held up her hand. There was instant silence. "Now, little folk," she said, "I am going to tell you how the Wax Flower brought joy into the heart of a little girl I know."

"Not long ago, a dear little girl lived on a farm in the back country. Although she was only eight years of age, she had to attend school—a distance of three miles. She had to walk all the way, because horses could not be spared from the farm. Poor, wee mite, she led such a miserable life. She had no one to walk home with her, and was so lonely, that her heart was often very, very sad.

THREE OF THE LITTLE GIRL'S FINGERS WERE BADLY INJURED.

"One morning, she came late to school, and her teacher, of course, wanted to know the reason. The little girl showed her hand, which had a piece of dirty linen wrapped around it. The cloth was so rough and loose, that the teacher took it off. She was very shocked to see that three of the little girl's fingers were badly injured. The teacher now learned that her pupil's hand had been caught between the teeth of a rabbit-trap. The poor child had to rise at daylight to visit the traps. The rabbits caught during the night were killed, and skinned, the traps re-set, and the skins brought back to the farmhouse. At sundown, the same round was made, and the same duties were done.

"As there were signs of blood-poisoning, the teacher drove her charge home, and told her parents about the danger. They had given little care, and less thought, to the injury, but said that they would give it more attention. They were, however, so half-hearted over the matter that the fingers rapidly became worse. In a very short time, the poison had spread beyond the hand. Indeed, the child's arm was red and sore to the elbow.

"The teacher, without delay, drove her pupil to the small township where a doctor lived. He would not, however, treat the case. He placed the little sufferer in the hospital, where she would be in the hands of a nurse. For several days, the arm was in great danger. Indeed, it seemed that the arm must be cut off. At last, however, the poison was taken away, and the hand, though very sore and tender, began to heal slowly. But it was a very narrow escape.

"The nurse was very kind to the child, and gave her a bunch of Wax Flowers to help her to be happy. How the poor little girl loved the gift! Indeed, she showed such delight, that the nurse said she would give the child a plant to take home. When she was able to leave the hospital, she carried away the plant, and put it in her own small garden.

"By and bye, the Wax Plant grew beautiful flowers. Even the tired mother was not too tired to say how pretty they looked, and she allowed her little girl to put some of the blooms into an old glass jug which was placed on the table. Now, they looked so nice, that the mother thought she would bring out her best cups and plates. Well, when you have nice things on the table, you always want to wear your best clothes at meal-times. Indeed, the father found his cleanest collar and tie, the mother changed her dirty apron and smoothed her hair, and the little girl had such clean hands and face that you really would not have known them.

"Of course, beautiful flowers and clean things bring beautiful and clean thoughts. Beautiful and clean thoughts make one wish to see little people happy. In a little while, the father bought a pony. It was such a beauty. The pretty animal had a creamy tail and mane, and trotted along so gaily, that the little girl was never late for school, nor too tired to listen to her teacher.

"It was not long before girl friends paid a visit to the farm and they, of course, invited their little friend to visit their own homes. In the end, the child became one of the happiest little girls in the world. You now see how the beautiful bloom brought a desire for all that was good into the hearts of the parents of the little maiden whose life was made happy by the wonderful beauty and lesson of the Wax Flower."

The Black Swan

Part I

THE Queen of all the Fairies had just turned to ask one of the little men to bring her a small bowl of clear water. You see, it was warm in the cave, and the Fairy Queen had become very thirsty, Before the little man had gone a step to obey the wish of his royal mistress, there arose the sound of a sudden scuffle amongst the pixies. Two of their number were rolling over and over, and making such a dust that the lights became quite dim. The little folk were on their feet, in an instant. They formed a circle around the two pixies, and watched the scuffle with eager interest. The little men, however, were very annoyed, and, grasping the offenders by their small tunics, brought them before the Fairy Queen.

The Queen of all the Fairies tried to look annoyed, but there was a smile in her beautiful eyes. She, however, spoke very severely to the little folk, who, with looks of shame on their brown faces, sat down at once.

The pixies were now asked why they had shown such bad manners. One of them, with tears in his eyes, said that the other pixie had tried to take something from him. He was asked to show the cause of the scuffle. Taking a cardboard box out of his big pocket, he handed it to the Fairy Queen.

The wee fellow, who had caused the uproar, was told to stand in the centre of the cave. He, of course, looked very foolish, for the little folk made fun of him. But he should not have tried to take what did not belong to him.

The Queen of all the Fairies now lifted the lid with a smile that made her face look more beautiful than ever. She lifted out the shell of a sea-urchin from the midst of a number of leaves in which it had been carefully packed. "Where did you find it?" she enquired. "I did not find it at all," sobbed the Pixie, "Flora gave it to me!" "Well, well!" said the Fairy Queen, "and tea-tree leaves, too! What a coincidence, to be sure!" "What's a coincidence?" asked the Pixie. "Just listen, my wee friend, and you will soon understand what the big word means."

"Now," said the Queen of all the Fairies, "you have never surely taken notice of these small leaves, or you would know that they belong to a tree that grows on the border of a wide plain. In this plain is a hollow that is filled with water when rain falls heavily. The water stays there for weeks, and weeks, and ducks, pelicans, native-companions, spoon-bills, ibis, and swans, feed on the life that lives in it for that time.

"This Tea-tree was very fond of practical jokes, and resolved to play a trick upon a black swan, that, at times, sat in the shade of its branches. One day, she dropped a seed-pod on his head, while he sat there dreaming of all sorts of nice things to eat. How he jumped, to be sure! With a flurry and a scurry he popped into the water. You should have seen the splash. The water beetles fled in terror to the shelter of the reeds. Their tiny hearts beat so fast, that the very weeds trembled. The Tea-tree laughed and laughed until there was hardly a seed-pod left on her branches. She called to the Black Swan who had turned around, once he was safe on the water, that there was no need for fear, for it was only a seed-pod that had dropped on his head. But the Black Swan only looked at her with reproach in his sad eyes. Indeed, several

THE TEA-TREE DROPPED A SEED-POD ON HIS HEAD. WITH A FLURRY AND A SCURRY HE POPPED INTO THE WATER.

hours passed before he would speak to the Tea-tree. In the end, he smoothed down his feathers and made it up with his old friend.

" 'Can you tell me,' said the Tea-tree, on one occasion, 'why there are white swans as well as black ones?' 'Oh, yes!' replied the Black Swan. 'Of course, you know that black swans are peculiar to Australia.' 'Indeed!' replied the Tea-tree,' how do you account for that fact?' 'Well,' said the Black Swan, 'if you will promise me that you will not drop any more seed-pods on my head, I shall tell you!' The Tea-tree promised, and the Black Swan, after smoothing a few feathers on his glossy back, began his story.

"A long, long time ago, before you were born, all swans were white. One particular white swan was paddling down an inland river, when, all at once, he heard the sound of weeping. He made his way towards the spot from whence the sound came. You may imagine his surprise when he saw two rabbits, who were sitting on the bank, weeping fit to break their hearts. He, of course, asked why they were so sad, and was told that a Goanna had ruined their home. The reptile had taken up his abode near their house, and, at dusk, he would creep silently to the warren and carry off the baby-rabbits. They had lost their last baby-rabbit in this dreadful way, and were preparing to make a journey into a far country. But they were very, very sad—and, indeed, they looked it.

"The Swan was, of course, very grieved, and told the rabbits he thought he could help them. He made them promise to stay where he had found them. He said he would see his friends—the Seven Little Grey Men—and return as soon as possible. You see, he knew that the little men would help him, for the little men were always ready to assist folks in distress. The Swan told the rabbits to take care lest the Goanna should get them, and set off to the cave on his mission.

HE RECEIVED SUCH A THRASHING FROM OUR BEAKS AND WINGS, THAT HE FLED INTO THE BUSH.

"Several days passed before the Swan returned. Indeed, the rabbits thought he would never come. They packed up their things and were preparing to seek a new home, when their friend, along with six other swans, appeared on the scene.

"Strange to say, their feathers were now quite black. The rabbits were puzzled and somewhat afraid. The voice of the Swan, however, banished their fears, and they returned to the water's edge to learn the reason of this wonderful change in the color of the birds' plumage. 'Tell us,' said the rabbits, 'why your feathers, which were once so white, are now so black!' 'Well!' said the Swan, 'it is this way! When I reached the cave where the Seven Little Grey Men live, and told them all about your sad loss, they made me stay with them until they had thought out a plan for helping you.'

"First of all, the little men went out, one very dark night, and gathered some of the blackness from the very centre of the midnight. They put it in a large, crystal bowl, and stirred, and stirred, until it was so black, that, try as you might, you could not see an inch into the bowl. I was then told to bring six other swans. When we returned, we had the fluid from the crystal bowl poured over our feathers until they were quite black. They now looked horribly dull, and we were not at all pleased. However, when they had used all the liquid, they cleansed the bowl, and re-filled it with a crystal fluid that bubbled and bubbled like boiling water. This fluid was carefully spread over our plumage. When our feathers dried, they looked as if they had been polished. Indeed, we rather liked their black, glossy appearance, and enjoyed the novelty of the situation.

"We were now told to go back to the river-bank where you lived, and hide in the long grass until the Goanna came along. We were then to punish him so severely that he would think twice before he stole baby-rabbits for his supper."

" 'Oh!' said the Tea-tree, 'I now understand why the little men changed the color of your plumage! The Goanna, of course, would not be able to see you at dusk. If your feathers had been white he would have easily seen you, and kept away from the warren.'

"Exactly!" replied the Black Swan, "you are certainly wiser than you look!"

"Well!" said the Black Swan, "to continue my story, we waited for the Goanna to appear. Night was just beginning to fall, when the rabbits told us that their enemy was stealing along the track that led to the warren. We squatted close to the ground, and, as he passed us, we pounced upon him. He received such a thrashing from our beaks and wings that he fled into the bush. But I am sure we must have left many marks upon his body.

"The rabbits were very pleased. They thanked us, and asked us to stay to supper. We were, however, unable to do so. As we paddled homewards, we thought that our new plumage was more useful than the old one, and resolved to keep it. Now you know how black swans came into the world!"

"Your story is full of interest!" said the Tea-tree. "You must have seen many wonderful sights in your time!"

"Oh, yes!" replied the Black Swan. "We often go down to the sea. The sea contains many strange and beautiful things, but, of course, we prefer the rivers."

"I should love to see the ocean!" said the Tea-tree, "but I suppose one would soon become tired of so much water!"

"Oh, no!" replied the Black Swan. "The ocean holds many wonderful things, but none so wonderful as its gardens!" "Now, you are making fun of me!" laughed the Tea-tree. "Indeed, I am not!" said the Black Swan. "I should like to see them!" continued the Tea-tree. "That is easily managed!" replied the Black Swan. "You must give me one of your seeds, and I shall take it down to the ocean, and introduce it to a sea-urchin who is a great friend of mine. He often plays amongst the rocks, and will show your seed, these wonderful gardens of the sea. I shall bring the seed back to you, and then you will know that I have told you the truth."

The Tea-tree was delighted to learn that the world showed so many interesting sights. She promised the Black Swan that she would give him a seed whenever he desired it. "Tell me more about the ocean!" she said. "Are there trees and plants in the sea?" "I told you there were gardens in the ocean!" replied the Black Swan. "Of course!" murmured the Tea-tree, "my remark was a foolish one." "Then, there are plants of coral," continued the Black Swan. "Plants of coral!" said the Tea-tree. "I thought coral was a kind of stone!" "So it is!" replied the Swan. "I mean that the coral is often shaped like a plant. Indeed, the Queen of all the Fairies has two beautiful coral ferns—one on either side of her throne. You see, it was this way! A silver gull, who was one of the Fairy Queen's most trusted messengers, told his royal mistress that, on one of his errands, he had seen some wonderful coral plants deep, deep down in the blue ocean. They were so like delicate ferns, that he was charmed by their shape and beauty. He thought that the Fairy Queen would like to have them, but, of course, he knew that he would never be able to secure them. They were too deep down in the sea, and were too firmly fixed to a big reef to be moved, except by great force. However, when the Queen of all the Fairies heard that such things were in the depths of the ocean, she spoke to the Wind from the East, and asked him to find a way whereby she might get some of these wonderful coral plants. The Wind from the East had a long chat with the Ocean, and they made a storm that stirred the mighty sea to its very depths. Great masses of water dashed against the reef, broke off a number of the coral plants, and washed them ashore.

As the Gull had said, these plants of coral were very delicate and very beautiful. They were so scarlet, that their color was even brighter than ripe quandong-berries. Of course, they were very heavy, and it took a number of fairies to carry them to the palace of the Fairy Queen. She, at once, placed two of them near her throne—one on either side. They did, indeed, look very beautiful, and the Queen of all the Fairies said she was charmed to have them.

Now, as you know, there is nothing that pleases the Fairy Queen so much as beautiful colors. Scarlet was her favorite color. She knew, of course, that the little men had already made the color live for ever, and she paid them the compliment of imitating their efforts. The Fairy Queen now, with the greatest care and skill, took the scarlet tint from the coral, and spread it over the petals of some wild flowers whose clear yellow color had often given her great delight. She thought, of course, that it would be a pity to do entirely away with the yellow tint. She therefore left a small yellow spot to show that she liked the former color of the flower. The rest of the flower became a bright, scarlet hue. If you should care to see the result of her work, you must look for a plant called the Scarlet Coral Pea. You will then see the measure of her success. But you must not miss the small, yellow spot.

"Of course, the coral plants were now quite white. Indeed, the Fairy Queen was at a loss to know what to do with them. At last, she gave them to the Seven Little Grey Men, who promised to use them to the best advantage. They ground up the coral to a very fine dust, and placed it in the crystal bowl. When the dust was taken out, it was spread far and wide over the gullies, and the banks of the shady creeks. When the Spring rains caused all things to grow, there sprang up wonderful ferns, looking, for all the world, like green coral. The next time you wander through the gullies, you will see these beautiful ferns and marvel at the skill of the little men.

The Black Swan

Part II

ONE day, when the water that filled the hollow in the plain had become too shallow and muddy to give the Black Swan his usual food, he took a seed from the Tea-tree, and sailed down the broad river to the mighty ocean. There were times when he flew, and times when he swam, but he never rested until he reached the open sea.

True to his promise, he sought the Sea-Urchin, and after introducing the Seed to his friend, explained the desire of the Tea-tree. The Sea-Urchin was only too glad to please the Black Swan, and took the Seed along with him to see the wonderful gardens that grew in the depths of the ocean. The Seed was charmed with the lovely beds of sea-grass. They had paths of the whitest sand running through them, so that it was quite easy to go from one bed to another. You never saw such vivid colors! Some were so pink, that the Seed at once thought of the blossoms he had seen in the bush. Others were so green, that the Seed declared the land never held such a color. Flowers of all hues grew in these beds. The Seed, of course, wanted to go up to a glorious violet flower and tell it how beautiful it looked. The Sea-Urchin, however, told his friend that it was not a flower at all, but a star-fish. He warned her that, if she touched the star-fish, she would lose her

THE BLACK SWAN FINDS THE SEA URCHIN.

life. The Seed was amazed. Indeed, it seemed impossible. But it was the truth.

There was one bed of such vivid scarlet, that the Seed went into raptures. When she heard that the scarlet flowers were really Anemones, she became silent with awe and wonder. Perhaps, what delighted her most of all was the number of gorgeous fishes that swam in and out of the water-palms. It really looked like a scene from Fairyland, and the Seed said "How lovely!" in soft and awed tones. And so they wandered on and on, until the Sea-Urchin said that it was time to go back.

Meanwhile, the Seed was surprised to notice that the waters above her were becoming rougher and rougher. The sea-floor had been steady when they set out on their journey, but, as they made their way shoreward, the Seed was tossed hither and thither until she became quite dizzy and ill. You see, the ocean had had a tiff with the South Wind, and had become so spiteful that it tried to wreak its anger on the sea-shore. Of course, that was very unwise, for the shore would not stand such treatment, and would not allow the waves to go too far. However, an angry wave would now and then manage to go further than the shore intended. The Sea-Urchin was unfortunate enough to be caught in one of these waves. He was hurled so far up on the beach, that try as he might, he could not get back. Worn out by his efforts, the Sea-Urchin lay on the sand. The rays of the sun beat upon his soft body, and he felt very faint. He saw the Black Swan in the far, far distance, but he was too weak to make his way towards his old friend. It was very sad to be so near, and yet so far.

As the hours sped, the Sea-Urchin grew worse and worse. He knew he must die. The Seed was, of course, in an awful state. She stopped laughing at the funny way the Sea-Urchin put out his tiny feet as he tried to drag himself along the sand. His efforts became feebler and feebler until at last, he lay so still, that the Seed wept with grief and fright.

THE OCEAN HAD A TIFF WITH THE SOUTH WIND.

Day after day passed. The soft body of the Sea-Urchin faded away until there was nothing left but his skeleton. The Seed gave herself up for lost, and was only brought to her senses by the sound of something tapping on the shell. A moment later, the shell rolled over, and the Seed fell out on the sand. You may imagine her feelings of relief, when she saw the Black Swan.

The Black Swan, who was in a terrible state of mind, had searched and searched along the beach day after day. He had almost given up the search in despair, when he spied a shell far up on the sand. You see, the Sea-Urchin had been hurled so far inland, that the Black Swan was unable to find him in time to save his life.

It was very sad, indeed, and the Black Swan grieved over the fate of his friend. He spoke kindly to the Seed, but she refused to go back to the Tea-tree. "I know the Sea-Urchin will return!" she cried, "and I shall stay here until he comes back to me!" The Black Swan sadly shook his head, for he knew better. However, he picked up the Seed, and carried her up to the top of the bank, where a quantity of coarse grass grew. He here placed the Seed so she could rest properly and get her proper warmth at night. With tears in his eyes, he bade her farewell, and promised to return in a few weeks, when, if the Seed had got over her grief, he would be only too glad to take her home.

The Seed, however, never wanted to return. By and bye, she took root in the spot where she had been placed by the Black Swan, and grew and grew until she could gaze down upon the place where the shell of the Sea-Urchin lay.

As time passed, other Tea-trees grew along the seashore. They are always watching and waiting for the return of the Sea-Urchin. You now know the reason why the Tea-tree grows by the sea.

"Now," said the Queen of all the Fairies to the Pixie, who had been made to stand in the circle while she told her story, "you may sit down!" The Fairy Queen really tried to look very stern, but her effort was hardly a success. Flora was smiling behind her hand, and the Queen of all the Fairies, unable to keep back her laughter, broke out into such a peal of mirth that all the little folk laughed too. Indeed, for a time, there was such fun in the cave, that you would have thought that all the laughter in the world was having a merry holiday.

When the mirth had ceased, the Pixie who had caused all the fun, quietly arose. He looked into the face of the Fairy Queen and said: "Dear Queen of all the Fairies, what is a coincidence?"

"Oh!" was the reply, "you asked me that question at the beginning of my story! Well, I meant to tell you all about the Tea-tree. The fact that there were leaves of the tree in the box, and the fact that, without knowing they were there, I intended to speak about them, was a coincidence. But you are a wise, little Pixie, and you may have back the gift you received from Flora."

All good things come to an end, and the Fairy Queen arose to depart.

"Good-night, little folk," said she.

"Good-night, Queen of all the Fairies," they replied.

When the glorious Queen had gone, the little men took the gaily-colored bowls from the walls, and, as each little brownie and pixie passed out of the cave, gave the wee mite one of the beautiful lamps. It was, indeed, a gift worthy of the occasion.

Should you ever go through the bush at night-time you will see lights dancing in and out of the scrub. These lights are carried by the brownies, and adorned the walls of the cave when the Seven Little Grey Men held their feast to celebrate the wonderful Crystal Bowl.

Again, the little men, who dearly love children, have asked me to tell you all about that glorious feast. With the help of Flora, I have told you what happened on that never-to-be-forgotten night. Flora says that the description is quite accurate, and that, if you are not sure what these long words mean, she will tell you.

Now, "Good-Night!" and remember that all these stories are quite true. Should you ever desire to know more about the wonders of Nature, you have only to ask the birds. They will tell the Seven Little Grey Men, who will whisper the answers into your listening ears.